By CYNTHIA LORD
Illustrated by ERIN MCGUIRE

Book 3

Shelter Pet Squad

Paloma

Scholastic Inc.

To Toni and Terry

Copyright © 2016 by Cynthia Lord
Illustrations © 2016 by Scholastic Inc.

All rights reserved. Published by Scholastic Inc., *Publishers since 1920*. SCHOLASTIC and associated logos are trademarks and/or registered trademarks of Scholastic Inc.

ISBN 978-0-545-63604-9

10 9 8 7 6 5 4 3 2 1   16 17 18 19 20

Printed in the U.S.A.   23
First printing 2016

The text was set in Janson MT.
Book design by Nina Goffi

Chapter 1

Shelter Pet Squad

"Hurry, Mom!" I said as our car pulled into the parking lot at the Maplewood Animal Shelter. "I don't want to miss the secret surprise!"

"I'm sure Ms. Kim and Ms. Flores will wait until *all* the kids in Shelter Pet Squad have arrived before they share the surprise," Mom said for the third time. "Have you finished your toast?"

I crammed another bite of toast with jelly into my mouth. I was too excited to be hungry, though.

1

Most Saturdays, my parents and I have a routine. When I wake up, I watch a few cartoons, and then we have breakfast together. After that, we get dressed and Mom or Dad drives me to the animal shelter. I'm a member of Shelter Pet Squad, a group of kids who volunteer to help the homeless pets at the shelter. With our leaders, Ms. Kim and Ms. Flores, we make fun things to keep the animals busy and happy while they're waiting to be adopted.

This Saturday morning was a little different, though. On Wednesday night, Ms. Kim had called my house.

"Could you come to Shelter Pet Squad early this week?" she asked. "We have a special surprise arriving on Saturday morning. Ms.

Flores and I could use extra help getting ready for them."

"Them?" I asked. "Are they cats? Dogs? Llamas?"

"Not llamas," Ms. Kim said. "But you don't want me to ruin the surprise, do you?"

Part of me *did* want her to ruin it. "Maybe just a hint?" I asked.

"Okay, here's a hint," she said. "This surprise is coming from an island in the ocean."

"An island?" I asked. "Is it monkeys?"

Ms. Kim laughed, but she wouldn't say anything else.

On Saturday morning, I got dressed as soon as I woke up. I tucked Whiskers, my favorite stuffed-animal mouse, inside my jeans pocket. He's little enough to hide in there and all anyone sees is a bump in my pocket.

The first time I met the other kids in Shelter Pet Squad, they all talked about the pets they had at home. I was the only kid without a real pet. So I told them I had a mouse named Whiskers. It was true and not true at the same time.

Now I wish I hadn't said that. The longer you wait to tell the whole truth, the harder it is to say it. I like having Whiskers with me, though. He's a brave mouse, and he makes me feel brave, too.

*   *   *

"Is that toast gone?" Mom asked as I hurried across the shelter's parking lot.

I took a last, extra-big bite as I pulled open the front door. I tried to say "yes," but it sounded like "yerg" with a mouth full of toast.

"Here's Suzannah!" Matt told Ms. Kim and Ms. Flores as soon as I opened the door. All the other kids in Shelter Pet Squad were already there, waiting. I could tell they were as eager as I was.

"Great!" Levi said. "Everyone is here!"

"Now can we hear the surprise?" Allie asked.

"Yes!" Jada said. "I can't wait anymore!"

"Okay, the surprise is —" Ms. Kim said, pausing dramatically.

"*Satos!*" Ms. Flores finished.

Ms. Kim and Ms. Flores were excited. But I didn't know what that was!

Luckily, I wasn't the only one. "Sat toes?" Allie asked. "What's that?"

"*Sato* is a nickname for a mixed-breed dog," Ms. Flores explained. "In Puerto Rico, there are many homeless Satos that roam the streets and beaches. Sometimes they're not treated well. Many of them don't live very long."

"That's so sad," I said. All pets need homes, and I'd do anything to have one of my own. We live in an apartment, though, and our landlord says, "No pets."

Ms. Flores nodded. "It *is* sad, but there are groups of people who help Satos. The rescuers leave food for the dogs and gain their trust. After the Satos are captured, a veterinarian gives them a checkup, and then the rescuers try to find homes for them. Some Satos are adopted on the island, but there are too many dogs and not enough families. So others are

7

flown in an airplane to shelters where they have a better chance of being adopted. My cousin lives in Puerto Rico, and he works with one of those rescue groups. He asked me if our shelter wanted to help. A volunteer, Mr. Lucas, should be back from the airport soon with six Sato puppies."

Six puppies! Wow! I couldn't wait to hold them!

"I love puppies!" said Allie. "They're so waggy and licky!"

"Can we play with them?" Matt asked.

"If the puppies *feel* like playing," Ms. Kim cautioned. "Remember, they've had a long trip, full of new sounds and smells. They might be tired or scared. Our first job is to make them feel safe and comfortable. While we wait for the puppies to arrive, I thought we could make each puppy a little bed. They can sleep on the beds while they're here at the shelter. Then, when they're adopted, we'll send the beds home with them so they'll have something familiar in their new homes."

I hadn't thought that the puppies might be scared or lonely. Satos were a wonderful surprise for *us*, but this was a new place and new people for them. They needed us to make them feel at home. A soft bed would be a good start.

That would be a nice surprise for *them*.

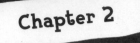

Getting Ready!

In the middle of the workroom table, Ms. Kim had put everything we needed to make puppy beds: flat, square pillows, a stack of big fleece squares, scissors, rulers, and a few pieces of chalk. "The fleece will make a covering for the pillow — like a pillowcase. We'll tie fringe around the edges to keep the pillow inside. First, everyone, choose two fleece squares," Ms. Kim said. "One square will become the top of the bed. The other square will be the bottom."

Some squares were solid colors. Others had patterns or stripes. I picked a square with a pattern of red with white paw prints for the top and a plain black square for the bottom.

"Now put your squares together, one on top of the other," Ms. Kim explained.

I lined up my two squares. "It's like a fleece sandwich," I said.

Ms. Kim gave us each a pillow. "Put this on top of your squares, right in the center. We want four inches of fleece on each side of the pillow."

When I had my pillow exactly in the middle, Ms. Kim gave us a piece of chalk to trace around the pillow. Then we took the pillow away.

"The chalk line shows us how far *up* to cut," Ms. Kim said. "Now we'll make fringe." She showed us how to lay the ruler along the edge of the fleece and make a little chalk mark at every inch all around the square.

Keeping the squares together, I cut slits of fringe through both pieces of fleece. One slit at each inch, from the edge up to the chalk line. *Snip. Snip. Snip. Snip.* It was fun!

Next we cut off the four corners. Then came the funnest part! Taking a piece of top and bottom fringe, we tied them together. I tied knots: one black fringe with one red fringe, over and over. "Be sure to stop when you've done three sides of the square," Ms. Kim said. "The pillow needs to go inside before we tie up the last side."

When I finished the puppy bed, I laid my head on it. It was soft, squishy, and cozy. A good place to rest after a long trip!

"Mr. Lucas should be here any moment now," Ms. Kim said. "Let's clean up quickly so we can get the puppies' pens ready."

After we put the materials away, I skipped all the way down to the dog kennel, carrying my puppy bed. I couldn't wait to see if the puppies liked the beds we'd made.

The kennel is a huge room with long rows of pens. As soon as we opened the kennel door, dogs started barking. We always have a variety of dogs waiting to be adopted: big dogs, little dogs, yellow dogs, black dogs, friendly dogs, and shy dogs. Ms. Kim knows every one of their names.

She had chew bones for the dogs. We walked up and down the rows giving one to each dog. Some of the dogs have been at the shelter for weeks. Buddy is a big, black dog that feels like an old friend to me. Every Saturday, it hurts to see that he wasn't adopted again. Ms. Kim always says, "Sometimes it takes a while."

"I have a bone for you, Buddy," I said, tossing it into his pen. "Happy chewing!"

Buddy wagged his tail. He started chomping right away.

Each pen has walls and a cage door, and inside is a dog bed and dog dishes and toys. But the pens nearest to the kennel door were empty. Each had a little whiteboard hanging on the side. The first board said, PAZ AND OSITO.

The next one said, MAYA AND ISABELLA.

PALOMA AND GIGI was written on the one after that. These had to be the Satos!

"We'll put two puppy beds in each pen," Ms. Kim said, putting the bed she'd made in the pen for Isabella and Maya. "The puppies have been traveling together, so they'll feel better if they have a friend to play and cuddle with."

"I bet it was scary to be captured," Matt said, putting his bed into the pen for Paz and Osito.

"And taken to a vet," Levi added, putting his bed in with Matt's. "My dog hates going to the vet!"

"Then travel in a crate. I bet they wanted to get out!" said Jada, adding her bed to Ms. Kim's for Isabella and Maya.

Allie and I put our beds in the pen for Gigi and Paloma. "And fly in an airplane!" Allie added. "Then ride in a van."

"And not understand what's going on," I said.

"Yes. This is all new to them," Ms. Kim said. "And they may miss what they've left behind. Paloma was found with her brothers and sisters in an abandoned garage. The puppies were curled up together inside an old tire."

"Are we getting Paloma's brothers and sisters, too?" I asked. "Or did they go to another shelter?"

Ms. Kim sighed. "The rescuers could only catch Paloma."

"They *left* them?" I didn't have any brothers or sisters, but if I did, I wouldn't want to leave them.

"The rescuers will keep trying for the others," Ms. Kim said. "That's all they can do. But here's what *we* can do. We can make Paloma, Paz, Osito, Isabella, Maya, and Gigi feel happy and loved while they're with us. We can find them good homes with people who will be patient and understanding. These puppies haven't had much experience living in a home. They'll need extra love and training. Let's give them a good start by making their pens cozy and fun, okay? There are lots of dog toys over in the toy bin."

"My dog loves balls," Levi said. "I'll choose a ball for each pen."

"I'll give each puppy a stuffed animal!" I said. "If I were a puppy, I'd want something soft to play with."

"I'll get them each a squeaky toy!" Matt said.

"Allie and Jada, would you help me fill three water bowls?" Ms. Kim asked. "The puppies might be thirsty. After they're settled in and comfortable, we'll give them some puppy food, too."

I dug through the bin of dog toys. There were lots of toys to choose from, but I moved aside any toys that seemed too big or hard or heavy. Puppy mouths are small. I made a pile of six little stuffed animals.

I put a soft toy cat in the pen for Gigi. For Paloma, I chose a floppy dog. Just in case she missed her brothers and sisters.

I gave Paz and Osito a stuffed lion and elephant. If they were scared, those animals might help them to be brave.

Maya and Isabella got a sheep and a squirrel with a long tail for them to play tug-of-war with. I was about to ask Ms. Kim if there were any real squirrels in Puerto Rico, when Ms. Flores's voice came over the intercom.

"The Satos are here!"

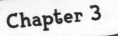

Chapter 3

Paloma, Surprise Package

"Oh, they're so cute!" Allie said.

Each crate had a door that you could see through. We all bent down to look at the puppy faces peeking out. The Sato puppies were different colors: white, brown, black, and some with patches of colors, but all with big eyes.

We watched as Ms. Flores carried the littlest crate inside the pen for Gigi and Paloma. I thought the puppies would come bounding out as soon as the crate was opened, but nothing

20

happened. Were they scared? Did they know they'd be getting a family and a new home someday?

I guess it might be hard to imagine something you've never had. I reached into my pocket and touched Whiskers. *Don't be afraid*, I imagined Whiskers telling the puppies. *Sometimes you have to go through something scary to reach something good.*

Then a little black nose poked out of the smallest crate. A tiny tan face came next. Then two little white front paws stepped out. "This one looks like she's wearing boots!" I said quietly as she explored the pen. I didn't want to scare her.

"That's Paloma," Mr. Lucas told me.

"How come they look so different?" Levi asked. "Osito looks like a beagle, but Paloma and Gigi look like Chihuahuas."

Gigi? I'd been staring at Paloma so much that I hadn't noticed the other puppy from the smallest crate. Gigi was just a little bit bigger than Paloma, but they looked very different. Gigi had long dark-brown fur, not at all like Paloma's short tan fur. Gigi was checking out the stuffed cat in her bed. I grinned. She liked it!

"Satos are mixed breeds," Ms. Kim said. "Looking at them, we can guess what breeds might be mixed together, but we don't know for sure."

Ms. Flores grinned. "Each Sato is a surprise."

"Six surprise packages!" Jada said. "It's like a birthday party!"

"Or a puppy party!" said Matt.

"Okay, Shelter Pet Squad, I have another surprise for you," said Ms. Kim. "If you put on booties and gowns and rubber gloves, you can go in the pens with them. These puppies were seen by a veterinarian before they got on the plane, but until our own veterinarian sees them, we want to protect them from any germs that might be on your shoes or clothes. And we want to protect *you* from any germs they might have picked up on their trip."

My heart was pounding with excitement. We'd never done this before. Ms. Flores gave us each blue cloth booties to wear over our sneakers, a yellow hospital gown to put over our clothes, and thin, white rubber gloves for our hands.

"We look like doctors!" said Jada.

"Paging Dr. Matt to the puppy pen!" said Matt.

"Here are the rules," Ms. Kim said. "When you go inside, sit down on the floor. If a puppy comes toward you, slowly hold your hand out with the palm up so he can sniff you. If he backs away or puts his tail down or doesn't come any closer, then he doesn't want to play and we'll let him rest and get used to his new home on his own. If he wags his tail or comes closer and tries to play with you, you can play with him gently and pat him, but not on his face or ears. No pulling or poking, just soft rubs on his back or on his tummy if he rolls onto his back for you. Only gentle playing, too. No tug-of-war with toys. Puppies play that game to see who the boss is, and if you play that game and they win —"

"They think they're the boss!" Jada said.

"Right!" Ms. Kim said. "I'll be watching to be sure everyone is being safe. But let's remember that it's been a long day for them. So we'll give them some space if they want it. Okay?"

We all nodded.

Matt and Levi went into the pen with the boy puppies, Osito and Paz. Jada picked Maya and Isabella. Allie and I chose Paloma and Gigi.

Inside the pen, I sat crisscross applesauce on the floor. Gigi went right to Allie and started chewing on her bootie. Allie picked up the stuffed cat, and Gigi pounced on it.

Paloma sniffed her water bowl. I giggled, because her bowl was almost as big as she was! I wanted to reach for her so badly that I had to sit on my hands to keep from doing it. Gigi seemed ready to play, but Paloma might not be.

As Paloma walked by, she turned her head to look up at me. Her eyes were dark brown and pretty.

"Hi," I said quietly. She came over to me, her tail up and wagging, so I slid my hands out from under my legs. My heart beat fast as I slowly reached one hand toward her, my palm up.

She licked my glove. It felt tickly. I bit my lip so I wouldn't laugh and scare her. Paloma didn't back away or look scared, so I patted her slowly with my other hand. Even through the glove, her back felt warm.

She pranced around me. She was so cute that I couldn't stop smiling.

I picked up the puppy stuffed animal and she jumped on it. Then Gigi leapt on it, too. Then the puppies pounced on each other!

"They are so funny!" Allie said.

I picked up the puppy toy and made it pretend to be running away. Paloma chased after it and grabbed it in her teeth. She flipped onto her back and held the toy in her paws, chewing it.

Gigi tried to take it from her and Paloma ran behind me with it. "Here, Gigi! I got you a cat," I said, grabbing the stuffed cat. Gigi pounced on it, but Paloma suddenly appeared from behind me without her puppy toy. She wanted the cat, too!

"They want whatever toys *you* play with," Allie said.

I kept picking up the toys and throwing them. Paloma and Gigi kept chasing them. They didn't bring them back, but Allie and I would reach for the toys and toss them again. It was so fun! The puppies looked cute jumping and running after the toys and trying to steal them from each other. I could've played all morning, but after a while, Paloma stopped chasing the toys and came over to me. She climbed onto my ankle and into the circle made by my legs. She yawned and lay down, her head on my knee.

My heart was beating hard. It felt like Paloma chose me. Maybe the circle of my legs reminded her of the tire where the rescuers had found her? As I moved my hand down Paloma's side, I whispered to her, "Everything will be okay, Paloma. You'll see."

She closed her eyes. Allie played with Gigi, but I was happy to just let Paloma rest in my lap. She slept there a long time, but then Paloma shuddered. Her paws were twitching, as if she was running in her sleep. She whimpered.

"Ms. Kim!" I said.

"What is it?" Watching Paloma, her face relaxed. "It's okay, Suzannah. She's just dreaming."

Paloma whimpered again. She didn't sound okay. She sounded scared. Was she remembering being caught? Or missing her brothers and sisters? "I think she's having a *bad* dream," I said.

"Speak to her gently," Ms. Kim said. "It'll wake her up slowly."

What should I say? When I had a nightmare, I always went to Mom and Dad's room and climbed into their bed. What did they say to me as I snuggled in with them? "It's okay, sweetie. You're safe here with me," I said softly to Paloma. "It's just a dream."

Paloma twitched and then her eyes opened a little. "You can go back to sleep," I said. "I'll stay right here until you wake up."

Her eyelids dropped again and she curled herself tighter between my legs. I let her sleep there until Ms. Kim put down a bowl of puppy food. That woke her right up.

Paloma stretched and then trotted over to eat beside Gigi. I'd been sitting still so long that my legs were all tingly when I tried to stand up.

"If all goes well, next Saturday will be adoption day for the puppies," Ms. Kim told us. "Our veterinarian will want to give them another checkup and their next round of shots first."

I watched Paloma crunching puppy kibble with her tiny teeth. She was so small and perfect. We probably wouldn't have her at the shelter very long. Everyone would want her.

But until then, she was mine.

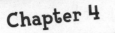

Chapter 4

Pet Day

Every Monday during circle time at school, my teacher lets us tell one piece of good news that happened over the weekend. Most Mondays, I have some good news, but this time I had great news! I couldn't wait to tell my whole second-grade class about Paloma and the other Sato puppies.

All weekend, I couldn't stop thinking about how fun it had been to play with Paloma. I also kept remembering her bad dream, and how I'd made her feel safe. She had needed me and I had been there for her. Maybe this was how it felt to have a real pet?

As Ms. Cole called us to circle time, I wondered what Paloma was doing right now. Was she playing tug-of-war and wrestling with Gigi? Or sleeping? Or maybe Ms. Kim was giving her a snack?

"Good morning, everyone!" Ms. Cole said. "Does anyone have some —?"

I put my hand up so fast I bumped my friend Claire next to me. *Sorry*, I mouthed.

"— good news to share?" Ms. Cole finished. "Dylan?"

I put my hand down. Ms. Cole doesn't let us keep our hands up while other people are talking. I paid close attention so I could try again the minute Dylan was done.

"My soccer team won its game," he said. "Three to two! It went into overtime. I didn't

think we'd win, but then Jordan kicked the ball, and the goalie tried to grab it. It went right by him!"

I tapped my fingers on my knee, waiting for my turn.

"That's good and *exciting* news!" Ms. Cole said. "It must've been thrilling for your team! Did you celebrate?"

Dylan nodded. "We went out for pizza!"

"How fun!" Ms. Cole said. "Who else had something good happen?"

My hand flew up, higher than last time.

"Rosa?" Ms. Cole said.

I sighed and put my hand down.

"My dad and I baked banana bread," said Rosa. "I used a masher to smush up the bananas."

"That's good and *delicious* news. I love banana bread," Ms. Cole said. "Claire, I saw your hand up. Do you have good news?"

Argh! When would it be my turn?

"My grandma came to visit and we went to a restaurant for lunch. Then we went shopping. I got new socks because I keep losing them." Claire lifted her pant leg to show off her neon-green socks. "Grandma said it'd be hard to lose these!"

"That's good and *bright* news," Ms. Cole said. "Who's next?"

My hand was up so high I was lifting myself off the floor.

"Suzannah?"

Finally! "On Saturday, we got some Sato puppies at the shelter where I volunteer. Satos are stray dogs from Puerto Rico. That's a long way, so these puppies had to fly on a plane to get here! They aren't used to living in a home, so they'll need extra love and training. Paloma is my favorite. The rescuers found her living in a tire."

Henry laughed. "A tire?"

I gave him a serious look, like Ms. Cole does when someone isn't being a good listener. "It's not funny."

"Yeah," Claire said. "It's sad."

I smiled at Claire. One of the best parts of having a good friend is always having someone on your side.

"The puppies had a hard start, but tell us the *good* news part of your story," Ms. Cole said.

"The puppies will get homes," I said.

Ms. Cole smiled. "That is good and *wonderful* news."

"My dog, Sparky, came from an animal shelter," said Tony. "But I think he just came from here, not Puerto Rico. Sparky needed training, too. He used to chew up my dad's sneakers — even when they were stinky!"

"My dog's name is Peaches," said Wesley. "She's a beagle."

"Remember to raise your hand to talk," Ms. Cole said. Just about everyone's hand went in the air. Estrella told Ms. Cole about her cat, Midnight.

"She sleeps with me every night," said Estrella. "Sometimes she sleeps wrapped around my head like she's a cat hat!"

"I have a rabbit named Leo," said Kennedy. "His whole name is Leo Funny Bunny."

"Pets are a wonderful thing to *write* about," said Ms. Cole. "During writing time today, you could write stories about your pets."

"Oh-oh-oh! I have a great idea!" Tony said. "After we write about our pets, we could bring them to school!"

"Well —" Ms. Cole started.

"Yeah! We could have a Pet Day!" said Henry. "Everyone could bring in their pets and read their stories!"

"I don't know if that would be allowed," Ms. Cole said. "Some people have allergies to animals."

And some people don't even have animals to bring, I thought.

"Does anyone have an allergy to pets?" Henry asked the class.

No hands went up. "See, Ms. Cole?" he said. "No allergies. Can we? Please? Please?"

"We'll see," said Ms. Cole.

With Ms. Cole, that usually means "no." Part of me was glad. It would have been fun to meet everyone's pet, but it wouldn't be fun to be the only person without a pet to bring.

Everybody else looked disappointed.

"How about this?" Ms. Cole asked. "I'll see what Principal Viera thinks."

"Principal Viera *has* to say yes!" said Claire. "It wouldn't be fair for him to say no when

Mr. Griffin's room has a class lizard. The lizard *lives* in his classroom!"

"And Ms. Janis's room has a bunny!" Mallory added.

"All right." Ms. Cole held up her hand, just like the crossing guard does for "stop." "I'll talk to Mr. Viera. If he says yes to Pet Day, your parents would need to bring your pet to school and then take it home again after a few minutes. We'd have to set up a schedule so the animals aren't here at the same time. Not all animals get along. Some animals might be afraid, too. So please consider if your pet would be happy coming to school."

Wait a minute. "We'll see" was starting to sound like "maybe," not "no," this time.

"What if your mom and dad are working and can't come?" asked Beth.

"You can bring in a photo of your pet," said Henry. He had all the answers.

"What if you don't *have* a pet?" asked Jemma quietly.

I glanced at Jemma. I was a little relieved I wasn't the only one.

"Then you could write about a pet you know," said Ms. Cole. "Maybe your grand-parents have a pet? Or your neighbors have a pet? You could even pick an animal that you see in your yard."

"We have lots of chipmunks in our back-yard," said Jemma. "Sometimes I put bits of bread down inside their holes. My dad says I'm like the pizza-delivery person, only instead of pizza, I'm delivering bread!"

"Fabulous! I can already see a great story there!" said Ms. Cole. "Everyone get out your writers' notebooks and start brainstorming ideas. This is a good day for writing about animals. Remember that stories need an interesting beginning, a strong middle, and a satisfying ending."

I went to my desk and opened my notebook. I did love to write about animals, but all I had at home were stuffed animals. I could write about Whiskers. I had already imagined lots of funny and exciting stories about him.

But when it was time to share, everyone would see he wasn't a real pet. I didn't want anyone to laugh at me, but I really didn't want anyone to laugh at Whiskers!

Maybe Paloma? I could ask Ms. Kim to take some photos of me with Paloma on Saturday before she got adopted. It wouldn't be the same as bringing in a live animal — an animal that was mine and loved me best, like

Peaches loved Wesley or Sparky loved Tony or Leo loved Kennedy or Midnight loved Estrella.

I was Paloma's in-between person. I was the "middle" of her story. Someone to comfort her and love her until she had a family of her own.

Still, that would be better than sharing a stuffed animal.

Or a chipmunk.

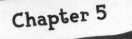

Chapter 5

A Wish

Mr. Viera said that we could have Pet Day in
our classroom as long as an adult was in charge
of each pet, and the pet stayed in our room. All
week during writing time, I worked on my
story about Paloma. Ms. Cole set the date for
Pet Day two Fridays away so everyone would
have plenty of time to finish their stories and
to make arrangements for their pets to come. It
was very exciting! Even though I couldn't bring
Paloma, I planned to ask Ms. Kim to take a
photo of Paloma and me together when I came

for Shelter Pet Squad on Saturday. I'd show the photo while I read my story to the class.

Looking at my story, I thought I had an interesting beginning. I liked my strong middle. But I didn't have a satisfying ending yet.

Paloma

I don't have any real pets, but I'm surrounded by animals. At home, I have lots of stuffed animals. Every Saturday morning, I also volunteer at the Maplewood Animal Shelter and help the real animals there. Since I started volunteering, I have helped a guinea pig named Jelly Bean find a new home in a classroom full of kids. I helped a ferret named Merlin find a home with a lady who needed a ferret.

Now we have six Sato puppies at the shelter. Their names are: Osito, Paz, Isabella, Maya, Gigi, and Paloma. They came all the way from Puerto Rico. My favorite puppy is named Paloma. The rescuers found her living in a tire with her brothers and sisters. They could only catch her, though. They took Paloma to a veterinarian. Then she flew on a plane and rode in a van to get here. I don't know if that was exciting or scary or fun for her. Probably it was all three things!

After I played with Paloma, she climbed into my lap and went to sleep. I was patting her and she had a bad dream. At first, I didn't know what to do! Then I talked to her and told her it would all be okay. I made her feel better.

On the day she was ready to be adopted . . .

(To be continued)

What would my satisfying ending be? I wouldn't know until Saturday. Maybe Paloma would be adopted by a family full of kids.

Or maybe a lonely person who needed someone to love would adopt her.

Or maybe someone would adopt Gigi and Paloma together.

I wanted Paloma to have a new home, but I'd miss her. What if she had a nightmare? I wouldn't be there to comfort her.

On Saturday, I asked Mom to take me to the shelter early. I brought Mom's camera with me. "Ms. Kim, would you take a photo of me with Paloma?" I asked as soon as I arrived. "We have Pet Day in my class and I wrote a story about her."

"Sure," Ms. Kim said. "Come down to the kennel. Maybe you could go in Paloma's pen and sit down? Then I'll take your photo holding her."

As soon as Paloma and Gigi saw me, they both stood on their hind legs with their paws on the pen door, trying to reach us. *Yip! Yip! Yip!*

47

"Good thing you didn't want a *video* instead of a photo," Ms. Kim said, laughing. "It would be a loud one!"

Gigi and Paloma pushed each other, trying to fit into the space where the pen door would open.

"Back up," Ms. Kim told them. When she opened the door, Paloma and Gigi squeezed through the space and got out! Ms. Kim caught Gigi, but Paloma ran right between my legs.

Oh, no! "I'll get her!" I took off running after her down the line of pens. Dogs started jumping and barking in their pens as Paloma and I ran past, as if they were cheering us on!

Lucky for me, Paloma stopped to sniff a broom just long enough for me to grab her. "Where did you think you were going?" I asked, scooping her up into my arms.

She licked my face, her tail wagging.

"She looks great in your arms," Ms. Kim said, putting Gigi back in the pen. "Let's take the photo right here."

Ms. Kim had to take several photos before we had one where Paloma was looking forward. She handed me the camera so I could see. In the photo, Paloma's mouth was open a little, like she was smiling. Her tail was a little blurry because it was wagging.

I liked that, though. It showed that she was happy.

It was hard for me to put her in the pen. Paloma whined and jumped against the door. She didn't understand why I was leaving.

"She's fine," Ms. Kim said. "It's only for a little while and then maybe she'll find a home today."

I wanted to be happy about that, but I really wished she could be mine. Paloma's brown eyes looked right at me, as if she wished that, too. "I'll be back as soon as I can," I told her.

When the other kids arrived, they were surprised that I was there first, because I usually get there last.

"We have Pet Day at school. I don't have a pet to bring, so I'm writing a story about Paloma to show my class," I explained. "I came early so Ms. Kim could take my picture with her."

"Don't you have a pet mouse?" asked Jada.

My heart jumped. *Uh-oh!* I wasn't expecting that.

"Yeah, what happened to Whiskers?" asked Allie. "I thought that was the cutest name."

I tried to swallow, but my mouth was dry. "Um, he —"

"Did he die?" Matt asked.

I reached into my pocket and touched Whisker's nose. I needed his extra bravery right now. "Whiskers isn't real," I said quietly. "He's a toy."

"What?" Allie stared at me. "Why'd you lie and tell us that he was real?"

"I didn't lie!" I said. "I never said he was real. I just didn't say he *wasn't*."

"That's *practically* lying," Allie said.

I looked down. "I'm sorry. I didn't want to be the only kid here without a pet. Pets aren't

allowed in my apartment. So stuffed animals are all I can have." I pulled Whiskers out of my pocket. "*This* is Whiskers."

Everyone was quiet. I bit my lip so it wouldn't tremble.

"He's cute," I heard Jada say.

I looked up slowly. She was smiling.

"I have a stuffed bear called Benny," she said. "He used to be white, but now he's gray because he's been washed so many times."

"I have a stuffed porcupine named Prickles," Matt said. "His prickles are soft, though. Otherwise he wouldn't be very squeezable."

"Mr. Hugglesworth has been my favorite since I was a baby," Levi said. "He's a teddy bear."

Everyone looked at Allie. She sighed. "My favorite is Caramel the Camel. She even has her own blanket that I made her."

I smiled shyly. My stomach felt like when I'm swinging: up-down, flip-floppy. I'd been keeping Whiskers a secret for so long. I thought it would be a huge deal if the other kids found out that he wasn't real. Maybe they wouldn't even like me anymore — but they did.

Ms. Kim smiled. "I think Whiskers would love to meet the little animals that came into the shelter this week. Come, let's introduce them."

As Ms. Kim opened the door to the small-animal room, I wondered, *Could the little pets be hamsters? Gerbils? Rabbits?*

Inside the room, I saw a gray bunny in a pen. Two pretty blue parakeets were perched on a wooden rod in a cage. Ms. Kim led us to two glass tanks with screen lids.

Each tank held a few mice. Real ones!

The mice were so busy! They were racing around or exploring, and then suddenly they'd stop to scratch or sniff the air. Then they were off again!

I held Whiskers up so he could see.

"The boy who brought in these mice started with two," Ms. Kim said. "A boy mouse and a girl mouse."

"Uh-oh," Matt said.

Ms. Kim nodded. "The mice had babies. Before long, there were more mice than the boy could take care of. He gave some away, but he couldn't find homes for these five. Two boys are in this tank," she said, showing us. "Three girls are over here."

A brown-and-white mouse picked up a sunflower seed in his tiny paws, nibbling it all around. A white mouse was rubbing her paws over her face to clean herself. A black-and-white mouse had climbed to the top of the water bottle. She looked around, choosing where to climb next.

"They're so funny!" Allie said.

"They don't have names," said Ms. Kim. "Would you each like to name one?"

We all grinned. "Yes!" Naming animals was a fun part of being in Shelter Pet Squad.

"Can the boys choose the boy mouse names and the girls choose the girl mouse names?" Levi asked.

"Good idea," Ms. Kim said.

Levi picked the brown-and-white boy mouse and named him Chester.

"This one is Hershey!" Matt said, pointing. "He's the color of milk chocolate."

I didn't know which mouse to choose. They were all so cute.

"Let's call the white mouse Blizzard," Allie said.

Jada chose the black-and-white mouse on top of the water bottle. "She likes to explore. So I'll name her Dora!"

There was one mouse left. I looked at the little, black girl mouse. Her ears looked like teeny cups, so thin you could almost see through them. She was trying to climb up the side of the tank, running her paws over the glass. Her long nose was pointed straight up, twitching. There was only one name for a mouse whose nose led her into adventures. "Mine's Whiskers!" I said.

"Today's project is for our new mice," Ms. Kim said. "Let's bring them with us so they can watch."

Ms. Kim and Matt carried the tanks down the hall to the workroom. On the table were pumpkin and sunflower seeds, a bag of mouse food, carrot and apple bits, sandpaper, a big bag full of shredded paper, and some plastic balls that were full of holes.

"Wiffle balls?" Matt asked. "Are the mice going to play baseball?"

"No," Ms. Kim said. "We're going to stuff the balls with shredded paper and treats. The mice will have fun rolling the balls around, discovering the food inside, and making nests out of the shredded paper. So it's a toy full of fun things."

"Like a piñata!" I said.

We each chose a ball and touched the edges of every hole. If any of the edges felt sharp, Ms. Kim had sandpaper for us to sand them down smooth. "We don't want the mice to get scratched," she explained.

Then we pushed bits of shredded paper and

treats into the holes to fill up the balls. My ball looked messy when I was done, but I was sure the mice would like it.

"Matt and Suzannah, let's give yours to the mice for now," Ms. Kim said. "I'll save the others for later this week."

Ms. Kim lifted up the screen top, and I cupped my treat ball in my hand so I could lower it gently into the tank. I didn't want to risk dropping it on one of the mice. Whiskers was so excited that she came right over to check it out.

She climbed onto my wrist to sniff the ball!

I froze. I'd never had a real mouse on me before. Whiskers's little paws pattered across my skin. Then her tail dragged over me. It felt so slight, just a tiny touch. A giggle burst inside me. "It tickles!"

Blizzard pulled shredded paper out of the ball. Dora tried to climb on it, making it roll. Whiskers picked up a seed and began nibbling.

Just then, the door opened. "Ms. Kim, there is a line of people in the waiting room who want to meet the puppies!" Ms. Flores said. "Are we ready?"

"A line?" Ms. Kim said. "Quick! Levi and Matt, would you take the mice back to the small-animal room? The rest of us will go to the kennel and get ready to greet the visitors."

"Let's each make a wish all the puppies get adopted right away!" Jada said, crossing her fingers.

Allie closed her eyes to wish.

I wanted Paloma to be adopted. She needed someone who would love her and take good care of her.

But I didn't want her to leave.

I closed my eyes. *Please let Paloma get adopted, but not first.* A few minutes wouldn't hurt anything. She'd still get a home, and I could have a little more time with her.

Only half of that wish came true, though.

Chapter 6

Adoption Day

"Shelter Pet Squad, you can tell people all about the puppies," Ms. Kim said. "But if you can't answer a question, send people over to me. Okay? I'm going to open the kennel door now."

It was exciting to be there on adoption day. Paloma jumped up against the pen door, looking at me, wagging her tail. She looked like she didn't understand why I wasn't coming into her pen to play. I really wanted to.

It'd be okay for a minute.

I opened the pen door and slipped inside.

62

Paloma ran to me. She jumped up on her hind legs and tried to lick my hands. Then she rolled onto her back and pawed the air at me. "You want me to pat you?" I grinned and sat down so I could rub her tummy. "Who's a good puppy?"

Gigi walked by and Paloma flipped onto her feet and grabbed Gigi's tail in her teeth.

"Hey, that's not nice!" I said.

But then Gigi had her mouth on Paloma's ear. She yipped and jumped into my lap to get away from Gigi.

"See, you don't like it either," I told her. Paloma lay down in my lap with her head on my leg.

I watched people walk by: families with children, older people, even a police officer in uniform.

It only took a few minutes for someone to adopt Isabella.

Ms. Kim said, "Jada will walk out to the waiting room with you and introduce you to Ms. Flores. She will talk about what a puppy needs and she'll go through the adoption paperwork with you."

As I patted Paloma in my lap, the police officer walked by, holding Isabella. "She's such a dear little girl," he said, patting Isabella. "My children have all grown up, and my house feels too empty."

"A puppy will fill your house right up!" said Jada. "You can have her bed, too. That'll give her something familiar for her first night. Isabella is a wonderful puppy. She really likes to chase the ball. She hasn't learned to bring it back yet, though."

"I can teach her that," the man said. "She sounds perfect for me."

One puppy adopted. Five to go.

"I like your puppy," a little voice said. "She's really cute."

I looked up to see a small boy in a red T-shirt watching me through the pen door. "Thanks," I said. "Her name is Paloma."

"You're lucky," he said.

I opened my mouth to tell him that Paloma wasn't mine, but he was already walking toward the next pen.

Should I call him back? Paloma was resting in my lap. Part of me didn't want to disturb her. Mostly, I wasn't ready to give her up, though. Not yet. When the boy came past again, I would tell him.

An older lady stopped in front of the pen. She looked like a grandmother, with gray hair, a nice smile, and a big purse. "Oh, these two are so sweet! Which doggie is the little tan sleepy one? He looks like he's wearing tiny white shoes!"

"It's a she. Her name is Paloma," I said. "And this is Gigi with the longer hair. Gigi is really funny and sweet. She likes stuffed animals — especially cats. She's a great puppy!"

I felt a little guilty because I knew I was making Gigi sound more interesting on purpose.

Ms. Kim came by. "Would you like to go into the pen with them?" she asked the lady. "You can get to know the puppies better that way. Suzannah will introduce you."

When the lady came inside the pen, she woke Paloma, who stretched and climbed out of my lap.

But Gigi was ahead of her. She went right over to the lady, wagging her tail. "Hello!" the lady said happily as Gigi jumped up against her legs and licked her fingers.

As soon as the lady put her purse on the floor of the pen, Paloma sniffed it. Then she grabbed the handle in her teeth and tipped it over.

Lipstick, tissues, and a cell phone fell out. The lady patted Gigi with one hand and tried to repack her purse with her other hand.

Paloma squatted down.

"Watch out!" I said, but it was too late. Paloma peed right next to the lady's purse.

"Oh!" she said. I was sure the lady would never adopt her now.

When Ms. Kim opened the pen door, I noticed something. The lady's arms were full. She was carrying her purse and the things that had fallen out. Plus, she was carrying Gigi!

"I'm sorry about that," said Ms. Kim. "The puppies aren't housebroken yet."

"No problem. All puppies need to learn," the lady said. "Gigi is just precious. I'd like to take her home."

"That's wonderful!" Ms. Kim said, smiling. "Suzannah, would you carry Gigi's bed and walk this lady out to the waiting room? Ms. Flores will take it from there."

The lady had picked Gigi. It had happened just the way I wanted it to. So why did I feel bad? "Can someone else do it?" I asked quietly.

Ms. Kim looked surprised. "Um, okay. Levi, would you walk this lady out to the waiting room?"

"Sure!" Levi said, grabbing Gigi's bed. "Come with me."

After the lady had gone, Ms. Kim turned to me. "Is something wrong?" she asked.

"I want to see who gets Paloma," I said. "I need to know for my story. I don't want her to get adopted while I'm gone."

Ms. Kim nodded. "I see," she said. "Okay. Would you get me a towel so I can clean this pen?"

As I walked slowly to the towels, I felt

relieved. As long as Paloma was here, she was partly mine. It would be all over when she got adopted. I was glad that Gigi would be getting a good home and that Paloma would stay at the shelter just a little longer.

I held Paloma while Ms. Kim cleaned up her pen, but she was wiggly and wanted to get off my lap. When Ms. Kim was done, I gave Paloma her stuffed puppy toy. I wanted to play, but she sat down and yawned.

"She's had enough excitement for now," Ms. Kim said. "Come out of the pen, Suzannah. Paloma needs a rest."

I sighed as I stepped out of the pen. I didn't want to leave Paloma, but Ms. Kim was right. She looked tired.

Paz was adopted by a family, including the boy with the red T-shirt who had asked about Paloma. He and his brother both wanted to carry Paz to the waiting room. "I'll hold him for now," the dad said. "But he can sit between you in the car on the way home.

"We have a puppy! We have a puppy!" the kids kept singing.

Next it was Osito's turn. "I had two dogs and one died a few months ago," said a man with a beard, scratching Osito behind the ears. "My dog at home needs a new friend to play with. Would you like to come home with me, Osito?"

Osito licked his beard.

"I think that means yes!" said Matt.

When Dad came to pick me up at the shelter, several dogs and cats, the two blue parakeets, and four of the puppies had been adopted. Paloma and Maya were the only ones left.

"Let's put Maya and Paloma together," said Ms. Kim. "So they'll have each other."

"I wish they all had been adopted," said

Jada as Ms. Kim put Maya into the pen with Paloma. "Do you think they're sad that no one wanted them?"

Paloma was asleep, so Ms. Kim set Maya next to her. Maya plopped her head down on Paloma's back.

"They don't look sad," Levi said. "They look tired out."

"It's been a busy morning for them," Ms. Kim said. "Maybe Paloma and Maya will be adopted before we close today. Or maybe tomorrow. Until then, let's be happy for the animals that did find homes this morning — even Buddy went home! He's been with us a long time."

I was really happy for Buddy and the other animals, but I was worried that I'd made a mistake keeping Paloma to myself. She needed a home, too.

And it was my fault she didn't have one.

Chapter 7

To Be Continued

The day before Pet Day, I sat on my bed, surrounded by my stuffed animals. I opened my notebook and looked at the ending for my story about Paloma.

On the day she was ready to be adopted . . .
    (To be continued)

I was still thinking about last Saturday. I'd wished for Paloma not to be adopted first, but I didn't mean I wanted her to *never* get adopted.

I just wanted to spend as much time with her as I could.

Maybe Paloma was adopted after I left? Or maybe she was adopted on Sunday? Or on Monday, Tuesday, Wednesday, or today? She was so sweet and cute. Someone must've adopted her by now. It would make a better story if I had *seen* the person or family that adopted her, but at least my story would still have a happy ending.

"Can you take me to the shelter?" I asked Mom.

She looked up from paying bills. "Today?"

I nodded. "It's for school. I need an ending for my story. I need to know who adopted Paloma. When an animal gets adopted, Ms. Flores usually takes a photo of the family. That photo will help me describe them. Please?"

"Well, I do have to go to the grocery store,"

Mom said. "Maybe we can stop at the shelter on the way?"

"Great!" I rushed back to my room to grab my story. I could write the ending at the shelter. That way I wouldn't need to remember everything that Ms. Flores and Ms. Kim told me about the person who adopted Paloma. I could write the end right there on the spot!

But when I rushed through the front door of the Maplewood Animal Shelter with my story and pencil, I couldn't believe my eyes. Paloma was in a circular portable pen in the waiting room. Shadow and Hattie, the waiting-room cats, were lying in chairs on the other side of the room, keeping their distance. Up on the bookcase, Hope, the goldfish, was swimming in her tank.

"Suzannah!" Ms. Flores said, coming from behind the counter. "What a nice surprise!"

Paloma jumped up against the side of the pen when she saw me, her tail wagging.

"I came to ask who adopted Paloma, but she's still here," I said, letting her lick my fingers. "How come she didn't get adopted?"

Ms. Flores shrugged. "Not everyone who comes in to adopt an animal is looking for a puppy. Maya was adopted this morning, though! And the two boy mice, Hershey and Chester, were adopted yesterday. "

I was happy for Hershey, Chester, and Maya, but I felt awful for Paloma. "She's never been alone before."

"I know, but don't worry," Ms. Flores said. "We brought her out here to the waiting room so she wouldn't be by herself. I can keep my eye on her, and everyone who comes in stops to play with her."

Mom put her arm around me. "I'm sure Paloma will find a home soon."

"Hi, Suzannah!" Ms. Kim said, coming out of the small-animal room. "Did Ms. Flores tell you that Chester and Hershey were adopted?"

I nodded. "And Maya."

"Yes, Maya has a wonderful new family." Ms. Kim smiled kindly at me. "And Paloma's turn will come, too. Most people who want a puppy come in on the weekends so they can bring their whole family with them." She reached into the pen and picked up Paloma. "Have a seat in one of the chairs, and I'll put Paloma in your lap. I'm sure she'd like to cuddle with you."

As Ms. Kim brought Paloma toward the chairs, we didn't even have to ask Hattie and Shadow to move. They jumped down and away.

Ms. Kim smiled. "Paloma tried to play with the cats this morning," she said. "But I don't think Hattie and Shadow knew what to do with a puppy!"

I sat down and Ms. Kim placed Paloma in my arms. I felt her heart beating under my hand. I laid my cheek on Paloma's head.

Holding her, I knew I'd feel a little sad not to see her again. But more than that, I wanted Paloma to be happy and have a home of her own. I was ready to do everything I could to make that happen.

"Pet Day is tomorrow," I told Ms. Kim. "And I have an idea! I'm going to tell everyone in my class about Paloma needing a home. Maybe someone they know is looking for a puppy. And I'm going to ask our principal if I can make a poster about her to put on the front

door of the school. Everyone who comes into school will see it."

Ms. Kim smiled. "That's a wonderful idea."

"If Paloma gets adopted before my turn at Pet Day tomorrow, would you call my school and leave a message for my teacher, Ms. Cole? It will change the end of my story. I want to get it right."

"What time is your turn?" Ms. Kim asked.

"I'm the last one before lunch," I said. "Eleven thirty."

Mom wrote down the school name and phone number for her. "I promise," Ms. Kim said.

That night, I made a poster. I titled it *Paloma Needs a Home.* I glued the photo of me with Paloma onto it. At the bottom, I wrote, *If you're looking for a funny, amazing, adorable, sweet, lovable puppy, Paloma is available at the Maplewood Animal Shelter. She's waiting for YOU.*

On my story, I erased the words *to be continued.* Ms. Cole always says the ending to a story is important. I had to write one, even if it might change.

On the day she was ready to be adopted, lots of people came to the shelter. Isabella went home with a police officer. *A lady adopted Gigi. Paz went to a family with kids. A man took Osito.*

Only Maya and Paloma were left. Then Maya found a home.

Paloma is still waiting for hers.

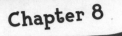

Chapter 8

Paloma Needs a Home

On Pet Day, I waited while Brayden showed everyone his lizard, Rodney. "He's a leopard gecko," Brayden explained as he took Rodney out of his carrier. "Leopard geckos are nocturnal, so he's usually asleep in the daytime and awake at night." He put Rodney on his arm and brought him around so we could all see.

Rodney was cute. He was yellowish green with black spots. He did a funny little waddle walk up Brayden's arm. "Rodney is quiet and

usually calm, but if I put him down, he can run really, really fast!" Brayden said.

"Please don't put him down," Ms. Cole said.

I thought a leopard gecko would be a fun pet, until Brayden said, "Rodney's favorite foods are crickets and mealworms. They have to be alive, though. Rodney won't eat them if they're dead."

I made a face. Even if Rodney was cute, I didn't want a pet that ate live things.

Three kids brought in their cats. We got to pat two of them, but Estrella's cat, Midnight, didn't want to come out of her pet carrier. So we just looked at her through the carrier door.

Wesley's beagle, Peaches, knew some tricks. I loved watching her dance on her back feet, roll over, and give "high fives." Colin's chocolate Lab barely let anyone pat her. She was so excited she just raced from person to person. Then she tried to steal Tony's lunch box!

As the morning continued, I felt better about not having an animal to bring. Some kids who had animals at home couldn't bring them in. I sat quietly while Ava showed a video she made about her backyard chickens. Nora had a big fish tank at home — way too big to bring to school — and she showed us lots of pictures she'd drawn of the different fish.

I even loved Jemma's funny stories about her backyard chipmunks. "They especially like trail mix," she said. "I have a little doll's picnic table, so I set it up on a stump outside and put trail mix on it. A chipmunk sat on top of the picnic table and filled up his cheeks with trail mix! He looked like this!" Jemma puffed out her cheeks as big as she could. "Another time, a chipmunk was trying to stuff a pinecone down his burrow, but the pinecone was too big and it got stuck in the opening. It looked like a pinecone was growing out of the ground! Even though they aren't pets," Jemma finished, "they're fun to watch."

"Thank you, Jemma," Ms. Cole said. "That was wonderful. Suzannah, it's your turn now."

I got my poster from the coatroom. The class said, "Aww," when I turned it around and they saw the photo of Paloma and me.

I picked up my story and began to read, "*I don't have any real pets, but I'm surrounded by animals. At home, I have lots of stuffed animals. Every Saturday morning, I also volunteer at the Maplewood Animal Shelter and help the real animals there. Since I started volunteering —*"

"OH!" the class gasped.

I looked up. Even Ms. Cole was looking at something behind me.

I turned around. I could not believe what I saw! Ms. Kim was standing in the doorway to our classroom with Paloma in her arms!

"I'm glad I'm not too late!" Ms. Kim said. "Suzannah, we took a nice photo of you with Paloma. But I knew you'd rather show your classmates the real thing."

I grinned. "Thank you!" What a great surprise! I could share my Shelter Pet Squad experience with my whole class!

86

Ms. Kim set Paloma down. She ran from one kid to another, her tiny tail wagging.

"Oh, she's great!" said Henry as Paloma grabbed his shoelace in her teeth.

Then Paloma jumped up against Claire's leg. Claire leaned down so Paloma could give her a kiss. "Suzannah, she's adorable!"

"She's my favorite," I said. Paloma wasn't mine for keeps, though. I needed to make sure everyone else knew it, too. "She came all the way from Puerto Rico," I explained. "And she's available for adoption at the Maplewood Animal Shelter. Right, Ms. Kim?"

"Yes," Ms. Kim said.

"So if your family is looking for a puppy, Paloma needs a home," I said. "She'd be a great —"

Paloma squatted.

"Oh, no!" I yelled, but it was too late. Suddenly, there was a little puddle on the floor.

Just when I thought things couldn't get any worse, they did! My yelling scared Paloma. She turned and ran right between Henry and Ms. Cole. She darted under desks and between the table and the trash can. Before I could even move to grab her, she ran through the classroom doorway and into the hall!

We couldn't lose her! "Paloma!" I called, hurrying after her. "Come back!"

She ran down the hallway, past the cafeteria doors. Her feet slid on the shiny floors, but that didn't slow her down enough for me to grab her. My heart was thumping almost as loudly as the footsteps behind me.

I turned to peek. Ms. Kim, Ms. Cole, and my whole class were running down the hallway with me. Everyone was trying to catch the puppy!

Ahead, the kindergartners were lining up to go outside. "Watch out! Runaway puppy!" I called to them as I passed.

A group of first graders crowded in their classroom doorway to see what was going on. "No running in the hallway!" one called.

"Even the teacher is running!" another said.

It looked like Paloma was going into the art room, but then she turned a corner.

Now she was heading toward the front door! What if someone opened the door and she got out? We might never catch her! My breath stuck in my throat. She'd lived as a stray before she came to us. I couldn't let that happen again.

I ran as fast as I could around the corner. The hallway ahead was empty. *Where did she go?* I stopped and looked in all directions. Ms. Kim, Ms. Cole, and the kids in my class spread out to look for her, too. But we didn't see her anywhere. She was gone!

Then we heard a deep voice. "What's going on here? Ms. Cole, is this one of your students?"

I gasped. Principal Viera appeared in the doorway to his office.

He was holding Paloma.

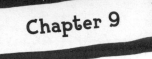

Chapter 9

Another Surprise

Paloma chewed on Principal Viera's tie. "Hey!" he said, pulling it out of her mouth. "Is this your puppy, Suzannah?"

I shook my head. "She's from the Maplewood Animal Shelter. I volunteer there. Ms. Kim brought her to Pet Day for me."

"Nice to meet you." Ms. Kim held out her hand, but Principal Viera's hands were full with Paloma so they just nodded at each other instead. "I'm sorry," Ms. Kim said. "I forgot to shut the classroom door when I came in."

"No, it was my fault," I said. "Paloma is just a puppy and she peed. I yelled and it scared her. That's why she ran." I looked at Principal Viera. "Paloma came to us all the way from Puerto Rico. She didn't have a home there. The rescuers found her living in a tire."

"In a tire?" Principal Viera patted Paloma in his arms. "Poor little pup."

"She rode on a plane and in a van with five other puppies to our shelter. On Saturday, all the puppies except Maya and Paloma got adopted. Then Maya was adopted yesterday. Paloma is the only one left." I paused. I knew I could stop the story there, but I'd learned my lesson with Whiskers. It's best to tell the whole truth right away — even when it's hard. "It was my fault Paloma didn't get a home. A lady liked Paloma, but I talked her into adopting Gigi instead. I wanted more time with Paloma because I wasn't ready to give her up. But I didn't mean *this* much time."

I peeked at Ms. Kim, afraid she'd look disappointed in me.

She smiled. "Gigi needed a home, too," Ms. Kim said kindly. "You helped her get one. We'll find Paloma a home. You know that sometimes it just takes a while for us to find the right match."

I nodded.

"Paloma, you came all the way from Puerto Rico?" I heard Principal Viera ask. "That is such a long way."

Paloma licked Principal Viera's chin.

"Paloma, do you know that my parents came from Mexico?" Principal Viera asked. "That's a long way, too. I was only a baby when my parents first arrived here. It was very hard for my family, because everything was new. Some people helped us, just like Suzannah is helping you."

I didn't know that about Principal Viera. He was in charge of everything at school. It was hard to imagine him as a baby. Or needing help with anything.

Paloma yawned and nuzzled against Principal Viera's neck. He sighed. "My kids have been asking for a puppy, but we live in a small house. How big will Paloma be when she's all grown up?" he asked Ms. Kim.

My heart jumped.

"We can tell that she's part Chihuahua," Ms. Kim said. "And at least one other breed mixed in. Since we don't know for sure, we can only guess."

"She's a surprise package!" I said. "Isn't that right, Ms. Kim?"

Ms. Kim nodded. "A puppy surprise package."

Principal Viera tipped his head, like he was thinking. I slid my hands behind my back, crossed my fingers, and wished hard. *Please!*

"I *do* like surprises," he said. "Ms. Kim, can I bring my family by the shelter tomorrow morning so they can meet her?"

"Of course!" said Ms. Kim.

"The shelter opens at ten o'clock on Saturdays!" I added.

Paloma licked Principal Viera's ear, making

him laugh. "I already know what my kids will say when they meet her. They will say, 'Can we bring her home?'" He smiled, handing Paloma to Ms. Kim. "Maybe I'll see you tomorrow, then." He winked at me. "At ten."

"Suzannah, let's bring Paloma back to the classroom so you can finish reading us your story," Ms. Cole said. "We stopped in the middle."

I'd forgotten all about my story!

Back in the classroom, I read every word, all the way to the end: "*On the day she was ready to be adopted, lots of people came to the shelter. Isabella went home with a police officer. A lady adopted Gigi. Paz went to a family with kids. A man took Osito. Only Maya and Paloma were left. Then Maya found a home.*

"*Paloma is still waiting for hers.*"

I looked up from my story. "But maybe not for too long," I added with a grin.

When it was time for Ms. Kim to leave, I asked if I could hold Paloma.

Paloma licked my cheek. "Be really cute when Principal Viera brings his family to meet you," I whispered into her little ear. "A home will be better than you can even imagine, Paloma. You'll have your own toys and your own yard and your own people who will love you. It'll be worth everything you had to do to get here. I promise."

Paloma looked into my eyes and wagged her tail.

I think she understood.

Chapter 10

Paloma's Second Chance

On Saturday, I woke up extra early, got dressed right away, and made breakfast for my parents.

"Wow," Dad said. "Thank you for the toast and bananas. What's the occasion?"

"I want to be at the shelter right when it opens," I told him. "Principal Viera said he might bring his family to meet Paloma. If they like her, she might get adopted right away!"

I put on my coat and sat at the breakfast table, watching Dad eat. "Okay, come on," he finally said.

When Dad pulled into the shelter parking lot, I saw Principal Viera, his wife, and his little kids already there waiting for the shelter to open. I was so glad I was there in time!

"Hi!" I yelled to them.

"We're getting a puppy!" his daughter said.

"Maybe," Mrs. Viera cautioned. "Let's meet her first."

"You're going to love her!" I called to her, because I knew they would. "Paloma is the best puppy ever!"

I knocked on the shelter door and Ms. Kim came to unlock it. "Hi, Suzannah! You're early today," she said.

"Principal Viera and his family are here to meet Paloma!" I said.

Ms. Kim smiled. "That's great!" She waved to them. "Come on in!"

As soon as I stepped into the waiting room,

Paloma wagged her tail and stood up on her hind legs, her paws against the side of the pen. I knelt down and held out my hand so she could lick my fingers. "Be yourself," I whispered to her. "You're perfect for them. They just don't know it yet."

"So nice to see you again, Principal Viera," said Ms. Kim.

Two kids, a girl and a boy, ran up beside me.

"Would you like to meet Paloma?" I asked the children. "Sit down on the floor, crisscross applesauce. Then hold your hand out with your palm up." I showed them how. "So she can sniff you. Let her come to you, okay?"

They both sat down, and I opened the pen. Paloma came right to me, but I turned her around gently, so she'd face the children. She sniffed and licked the little girl's hand and then climbed into the little boy's lap.

"She likes us!" he said.

"And we love her!" the little girl said. "Can we keep her? I've always wanted a puppy, and she's my dream come true! Please?"

"Please! Please!" the little boy said.

"Well, what do you think?" Principal Viera asked his wife.

She smiled. "I think we have a dog!"

I knew this family would love her and take good care of her. "I made Paloma a fleece bed,"

I told Principal Viera. "You can take it home with you. So she'll have something familiar."

"Thank you," Mrs. Viera said.

"And if she has a nightmare, just speak softly to her and tell her it'll be okay. That will make her feel better," I told the children.

"I'll say, 'Don't be sad, Paloma,'" the little boy said, patting her gently.

The rest of the Shelter Pet Squad kids arrived while Principal Viera was filling out the adoption paperwork. I told them the story. "And then, right in the middle of my reading at school, Ms. Kim came in with Paloma!"

"Wow!" Jada said.

"But that wasn't the biggest surprise," I continued. "Ms. Kim put Paloma down and she peed! I yelled and it scared her. That's when she ran out of the classroom!"

"We forgot to shut the door," Ms. Kim added.

"We all tried to catch her, but Paloma ran down the hall — right into Principal Viera's office." I grinned. "Paloma made her own match!"

"I'll bring her to school to visit your class again, Suzannah," Principal Viera said. "After she's housebroken, that is!"

My heart felt like a balloon, full almost to popping. Paloma had a family now, and sometimes she'd have a whole classroom full of kids to play with — including me.

As Principal Viera carried Paloma to his car, I stood at the shelter window and watched his kids skipping across the parking lot. I felt only a tiny drop of sad. The sort of sad when something wonderful happens for a good friend, and you have to let her go.

Through the window, I saw Principal Viera wave to someone as he climbed into his car. I looked over and said the first thing that came to my brain. "It's my teacher!"

What was she doing here? I hurried to open the front door for Ms. Cole.

She smiled. "Suzannah, you've inspired me. Every Monday morning, I love hearing your good news about the shelter animals. So I had an idea. It will be *my* good news on Monday."

"What?" I asked.

"Some of the other teachers at school have classroom pets," Ms. Cole said. "Since no one has allergies in our class, I thought maybe we could have one, too. It has to be a small pet, though. Something that's not too noisy. Something that will be easy for us to care for as a class. What do you suggest?"

"I know just the pet!" I said. "Come with me!" Ms. Cole, Ms. Kim, and the kids in Shelter

Pet Squad all followed me into the small-animal room.

Ms. Cole liked the bunny, but when she got to the tank of girl mice, she laughed out loud. Dora had climbed on top of the wheel and was rocking back and forth. Blizzard was hiding in a nest of shredded paper, with just her tail sticking out. Whiskers came right over to see us, her nose in the air.

"Mice are mostly quiet," Levi said, behind us.

"They aren't hard to take care of," Allie said. "You just have to clean the tank and make sure they have food and water and safe toys to play with."

"I can show our class how to make fun things to keep them happy and busy," I added.

Ms. Cole smiled. "That sounds perfect. How much do they cost?"

"The adoption fee is five dollars for each mouse," Ms. Kim said. "But if you take all three, I'll throw in the tank and everything inside it."

"It's a deal!" Ms. Cole said.

I grinned as Ms. Cole went into the waiting room to sign the adoption paperwork. A classroom pet was almost as good as having one of my own! And three classroom pets would be amazing!

I reached into my pocket. I had two mice named Whiskers now — a stuffed toy at home and a real mouse pet at school.

That was the best surprise of all.

Fast Facts about Dogs

- There are hundreds of breeds of dogs.
- The smallest dog breed is the Chihuahua, and the Irish wolfhound is the tallest.
- Over one-third of all American families have a dog living with them.
- In 2014, the most popular dog breed in the United States was the Labrador retriever, and the most popular names for dogs were Max and Bella.
- Dogs are nicknamed Man's Best Friend because they can form a very strong bond with the people they love. Dogs can also be trained to do jobs to help people. Some of the people who use trained dogs are: hunters, police officers, farmers, and people with disabilities.
- All dogs are direct descendants of wolves.

• Dogs have a sense of smell and hearing that is much stronger than ours.

• George Washington had many dogs, including one called Sweetlips!

• In their first weeks, puppies sleep 90 percent of the day.

• Puppies are born with their eyes closed. Their eyes open at about three weeks old.

• When a puppy turns one year old, he is considered an adult dog.

• The expression "You can't teach an old dog new tricks" isn't true! Dogs can learn new things at any age.

You can learn more about dogs
at the library and online.

Ways YOU Can Help Shelter Animals in Your Area

• Have a penny drive and compete with another class to see which class can collect the most. Maybe there could be a prize for the winning class, and all the money collected could be donated to your local shelter.

• Decorate a plain T-shirt with fabric pens, with drawings and slogans about shelter animals. When you wear it, people may comment or ask you about it. That will give you the chance to explain about the importance of adopting animals.

• Check your local shelter's wish list or ask if they use old newspapers to line cages. If they do, hold a neighborhood newspaper drive.

• Decorate Ping Pong balls with nontoxic permanent markers to make fun toys for shelter cats.

• Research how to interact with dogs safely and how to read their body language. Most people know that when a dog growls, he is feeling angry or upset. Did you know that any of *these* signals can also mean a dog feels stressed or threatened?

  • A stiff tail and/or a tensed body
  • Ears pulled back
  • Furrowed brow
  • Yawning
  • Backing away
  • Eyes moved back so you see the white parts of his eyes
  • An intense stare

• Make posters for your school to teach others how to approach dogs and read their body language, too. You just may save another student from a dog bite! Before you hang up your posters, be sure to ask permission.

• Suggest to your teacher or club leader that a veterinarian, dog trainer, or groomer could come in and talk to your class about how to safely interact with dogs and other animals.

• Show younger children how to be kind to animals. Tell a grown-up immediately if you see anyone not treating an animal kindly or if you notice the animal is upset.

No-Sew Dog Beds

To make a dog bed like Suzannah makes in the story, you will need:

- *Fleece fabric*
- *A simple flat pillow*
- *Scissors*
- *A ruler*
- *A piece of chalk*

1. Use the ruler to measure your pillow. How many inches long and how many inches wide is it?

2. Now add eight inches to both the length and the width numbers. That's how big to cut your fleece. You want the fleece to cover the pillow, plus have four inches of extra fleece all the way around the pillow.

3. Cut two pieces of fleece. These will become the top and bottom of the bed. If you cut the two pieces of fleece at the same time, they'll line up perfectly.

4. Put the fleece you want for the bottom of the bed on top. Place the pillow perfectly in the middle, so you have four inches of extra fleece on each side.

5. Trace around the pillow with the chalk. This will show you how far *up* to cut fringe. Then remove the pillow.

6. Place the ruler along the edge of the fleece and make a little chalk mark at every inch along all four sides around the fleece.

7. Keeping the two pieces of fleece together, make a cut at every one-inch mark up to the chalk line. This will make fringe that is one-inch wide and four inches long. Do this around all four sides.

8. Cut off the four corners, where the fringe overlaps.

9. Take a piece of top fringe and bottom fringe and tie them together in a loose knot. Do this around three sides of the fleece.

10. Before you tie up the fourth side, place the pillow inside the fleece.

11. Tie up the fourth side.

Give it to your pet to enjoy!

Plastic Treat Balls

To make a treat ball like Suzannah makes in the story, you will need:

- *A plastic ball with holes in it*
- *Treats for small animals (shredded paper, hay, carrot and apple bits, sunflower seeds, nesting material, etc.)*
- *Sandpaper*

1. Carefully check the plastic ball and all the holes for sharp edges. If you find any, use the sandpaper to make them smooth.

2. Stuff the ball with shredded paper, hay, and treats that little animals like.

3. Give it to your pet and watch him have fun.

4. If your animal starts to chew on the plastic ball, remove the ball.

Is a Puppy a Good Pet for Me?

A puppy can make a wonderful pet. Bringing a pet into your family is a big decision, though. Here are some questions your family should think about if your family is considering a puppy as a pet.

• Do you live in a place that allows dogs? Where will you walk and exercise your dog? Will anyone be disturbed by the dog's barking?

• Do you have time for a dog? Will someone be home with the puppy during the day? A puppy needs training and companionship.

• Do you have enough money for a dog? Buying the dog is only the first expense. A dog will also need food, veterinary care, training, grooming (depending on the breed of dog), and supplies like bedding and toys.

- How will your family feel about messes? Puppies will have housebreaking accidents while they are learning. Puppies also may chew things that don't belong to them. Most dogs shed or track mud into the house.
- Is anyone in your family allergic to fur?
- Are you willing to do some research before you bring a puppy home? Dogs come in many breeds and sizes. Each one has specific traits and needs. A companion breed will enjoy curling up next to you while you watch TV, but a working breed may get restless and want to be busy all the time. Finding a dog that matches your lifestyle is important for both of you.
- Is your family ready to train a dog? Dogs can learn many things, but they need everyone to be patient and to teach the same way. Are there puppy classes you can attend so you will learn how to teach your puppy what he needs to know? Bad habits like begging at the dinner table are easier to stop from the beginning than they will be to change later.
- Is there a baby or toddler in your family? Little children can do things that hurt or annoy dogs (hugging, pulling tails, etc.), and even patient dogs can get upset.

Both dogs and small children need to be protected from harm. If there's a baby or toddler in your family, it may be best to wait a while to bring a dog into your family.

• Are you willing to read books, watch videos, and attend classes to learn everything you will need to know to keep your pet safe and happy?

My family has had many pets. We've had gerbils, hamsters, frogs, fish, guinea pigs, rabbits, a cat, dogs, and mice. We didn't have all those pets at the same time, but over the years, we've shared our home with all of them.

I also volunteer at my local animal shelter. One day, the manager of the shelter called me and asked if I could help with some Sato puppies that were arriving on a plane from Puerto Rico. Just like Suzannah, I didn't know what that meant. So I went online and learned about Satos. I felt sad knowing that some of these puppies had been strays. Then I read about some organizations in Puerto Rico that help

Satos. It made me happy to know there are people working hard to help.

When our Sato puppies arrived, they were all different. Some were big. Some were small. Some were black and brown. Some were tan and white. Some had long hair, and some had short hair. My favorite puppy was a tiny tan one named Happy. He wagged his tail and climbed into my lap. I really wanted to take him home! But our family already had a dog, two rabbits, and a guinea pig. That's a good number of pets for us. So I helped care for the puppies, and I was glad when they were adopted.

I thought about Happy when I was writing this book. Just as for Paloma, Happy's hard start was the beginning of his story. The middle part was all the people who helped him: the Sato organizations in Puerto Rico, the people at the airline, and everyone at my local shelter — including me. The best part of Happy's story was the end, though. Just like Paloma, he has a new home with a family that loves him very much.

Happy got a happy ending.

You can learn more about me and see photos of the pets I have today at www.cynthialord.com.

–Cynthia Lord